NODDY
AND THE FARMYARD MUDDLE

by Sophie Smallwood

HarperCollins *Children's Books*

First published in the UK by HarperCollins Children's Books in 2010
1 3 5 7 9 10 8 6 4 2
ISBN: 978-0-00-736647-7

A CIP catalogue record for this title is available from the British Library.

Printed and bound in China

NODDY
AND THE FARMYARD MUDDLE

by Sophie Smallwood

Contents

NODDY DROVE THE CAR OUTSIDE, THEN SET TO WORK.
AS HE POLISHED HE SANG.

A TAXI TRIP FOR NODDY

ONE morning Noddy woke up very early. The sun was peeping through the curtains and the birds were calling to him.

> *"Wake up, wake up,*
> *Hop out of bed,*
> *Time to get up,*
> *Old sleepy head!"*

Noddy laughed and hopped out of bed, his head nodding happily.

"I'm not old and my head is not sleepy – look!"

He threw open his curtains to show the birds his nodding head. Noddy pulled on his clothes, put on his hat with the jingly bell and tied up the laces on his bright red shoes. After breakfast Noddy went to get his car out of the little brick garage he had built next door to his House-for-One. As he opened the doors, the sunlight streamed in.

"Time to give you a polish," smiled Noddy.

His car tooted cheerfully. "Parp-parp!"

Noddy drove the car outside, then set to work. As he polished he sang.

> *"Oh, the sun is bright,*
> *And the sky is blue,*
> *You shine so much,*
> *You look brand…"*

"PARP!" the car interrupted.

Noddy was so surprised he fell backwards, landing on the ground with a hard bump. He looked up to see Miss Katie Kitten. She was wearing a pink coat and was carrying a basket full of baby clothes.

"I am so sorry to bother you Noddy, but I must go to Toy Cat Town," she began. "My Auntie Furry is having kittens and she needs my help. Can you take me to the station?"

Noddy jumped up.

"Of course!" he cried.

Soon the pair were motoring along the winding streets of Toyland.

On their way to the station they passed a smart red cart. Farmer Straw was sitting in the driving seat in his best coat. At the front, his big brown horse Stamper flicked his tail to say hello.

"Good morning Noddy, hello Katie Kitten!" said Farmer Straw. "We're off to market."

Farmer Straw's two farm dogs, Shadow and Shep, were sitting beside him. They felt very proud to be driving to market in such a fine carriage.

"Hello Farmer Straw," called Noddy and Katie Kitten. Katie waved and the bell on Noddy's hat jingled merrily.

Everyone was so busy saying hello, no one spotted the two goblins standing on the other side of the road. No one heard them whisper to each other. The goblins, Sly and Gobbo, both grinned, their eyes round with mischief. As soon as Noddy and Farmer Straw went on their way, the sneaky pair held hands and crept over to the farm.

- 2 -

SLY AND GOBBO MAKE SOME MISCHIEF

SLY and Gobbo had always wanted to see the animals on the farm, but Farmer Straw's dogs would never let them through the gate – they knew just how naughty those goblins could be! Now Shadow and Shep had gone to market, there was no one to stop them coming in and doing as they pleased. The goblins laughed with joy as they swung on the gate. This was going to be such fun! The pair set off straightaway to find the animals.

The first thing Sly and Gobbo saw were some ducks swimming on the pond. As soon as they spotted the goblins, the ducks paddled over, calling

"Quack, wack, wack-wack." It almost sounded as if they were laughing! Sly and Gobbo started to laugh too.

"Let's find some friends for the ducks," sneered Gobbo.

His eyes flicked left and right, until he spotted a tractor parked beside the barn. It had been painted a beautiful, shiny red.

"Gobbo," said Sly. "Do you think that tractor can swim?"

In a moment, Sly had jumped into the seat. He made the engine roar. The naughty goblin pressed the pedals with his feet and turned the steering wheel.

THE TRACTOR REALLY DID NOT LIKE ZOOMING BACKWARDS

"Wheeeeee!" cried Sly, as the tractor started to chug backwards. Clouds of smoke bellowed out of the exhaust. The tractor really did not like zooming backwards. The out-of-control machine rushed down the bank, straight into the duckpond. The ducks flapped to the edge of the pond as the tractor hit the water with an enormous SPLASH.

The goblins squealed with laughter.

"Quick, Sly," said Gobbo, "let's go and find some more animals to play with."

The mischievous pair wandered over to the pig sties, pointing rudely at the animals' curly tails.

"Would you like a pig's tail, Sly?" sniggered Gobbo.

"No," said Sly. "But I'd like to see you with some cow's ears."

Gobbo shook his head. "They'd be far too tickly!"

"I know," whispered Sly. "We could turn the cows blue." Gobbo giggled at such a naughty idea, adding, "We could make the pigs woolly too!"

The goblins clapped their hands with delight. Sly pointed his long fingers over to the cows' meadow and sang.

> *"How now Mrs Cow,*
> *From your horns,*
> *To your moo,*
> *You'll turn completely blue."*

With a loud crack and a puff of smelly smoke the cows did, indeed, turn bright blue! The poor creatures were so surprised they didn't know what to say. They just stood like statues in the field, staring at each other.

Next, Gobbo pointed his long fingers at the pigs and skipped about, singing.

"This little pig had a tail,
This little pig had trotters,
Higgory, jiggery jig,
Now it's a woolly little pig!"

ZOING! At that moment, white woolly curls sprang out all over the pigs' bodies.

"OIIINK!" snorted the pigs.

The terrified animals shot round the farmyard, trying to escape their new fleecy coats. It was no good – the wool was stuck fast.

WITH A LOUD CRACK AND A PUFF OF SMELLY SMOKE
THE COWS DID, INDEED, TURN BRIGHT BLUE!

The mean goblins clapped their hands in delight. They had been naughty!

Farmer Straw's prize bull bellowed with rage. He had seen everything that had happened.

"How dare those goblins do such bad things?" he snorted. The bull lowered his head and charged.

"Look!" shrieked Gobbo.

"Time to go!" cried Sly.

The goblins escaped through the open gate and out to the road, followed by the bull and a herd of angry animals. The bull roared, the blue cows mooed, the sheep baa'd, the woolly pigs oinked, the ducks quacked and the hens clucked as they all raced after the troublemakers.

Before the farmyard animals could catch up, the goblins disappeared. Sly and Gobbo dived behind some bushes and hid there until the coast was clear. What would they get up to next?

3

NODDY THE SHEPHERD

THE farm was very quiet now. The gate creaked as it swung in the gentle breeze. On a high wall stood a lone cockerel. He had fluttered up there when Sly and Gobbo had started casting spells.

"Cock-a-doodle-do, what shall I do?" he crowed.

Suddenly the bird jumped down, fluffed out his feathers and strutted out of the farm. He had just had a very good idea. It was time to find Big-Ears!

While the cockerel marched along the road towards Big-Ears' toadstool house, Noddy was driving through the town. He had been very busy. First he had dropped Katie Kitten at the station and helped her on to the train. Then he had delivered a parcel to Mr Wobbly-Man. Now he was driving back from town with Mrs Noah. She had lots of shopping and needed to get back to the ark.

NODDY DROPPED KATIE KITTEN AT THE STATION
AND HELPED HER ON TO THE TRAIN

As they drove along the road, Noddy heard a funny noise. For a moment he was sure he heard someone calling out "Bath!"

'Who would want a bath out here?' thought Noddy.

They drove a little further, before he heard what sounded like "Bear!"

Noddy began to feel rather scared. 'Surely there's no bear down this lane,' he thought.

He drove carefully around the corner, not sure what he was going to see or hear next.

What a surprise! In front of them was a flock of fluffy sheep.

"Baaa!" they cried.

Noddy stopped the car so that he and Mrs Noah could climb out.

"Where have you come from?" he asked, scratching his head.

"They look like Farmer Straw's sheep," said Mrs Noah. She pointed at a very round creature wearing a pink ribbon. "That one is called Raggy."

Raggy stepped forward and nodded her head.

"Baaa!" she called. "Baaa! Baaa!"

"Well, I'm glad you aren't bears," said Noddy.

"You are funny Noddy," laughed Mrs Noah. "Of course they're not bears! We had better get them back to the farm though – Farmer Straw will be worried."

Noddy looked at the sheep and then turned back to his little car.

"They are going to have to walk," he decided. "I'll never fit all of them in!"

Noddy and Mrs Noah got back in their seats. When they were ready to go, the car beeped its horn.

"Parp-parp!"

The poor sheep jumped in fright. Some ran up the road and some trotted as fast as they could down the road.

"Oh, dear!" cried Noddy. "What are we going to do now?"

Mrs Noah stood up and took a small flute out of her pocket. She put the flute to her lips and played a beautiful lilting tune. The sheep came running up to her at once. Mrs Noah knew they would like it because she often played to the animals in the ark.

"Start driving Noddy," she said. "They'll be sure to follow."

Mrs Noah played the flute all the way back to the farm. When they finally drove up the lane, they found the farm gate swinging on its hinges. Noddy gasped at the empty yard. Then he saw the pond.

Instead of paddling ducks, it was filled with Farmer Straw's brand new tractor! Whatever had happened? Where were all the animals?

"Oh dear!" cried Noddy. "Farmer Straw is going to be so cross!"

Mrs Noah looked at the tractor.

"I'll go back to the ark and fetch Stumpy the elephant," she decided. "He can help us pull out the tractor – pushing and pulling is his favourite thing."

"That is a good idea," nodded Noddy. "I'll put the sheep back and then run to Mr Sparks' garage."

Noddy knew that if anyone could fix the soggy tractor, it was Mr Sparks.

"Bye bye car!" he shouted. "See you very soon!"

4

NODDY MEETS THE WOOLLY-PIGS

AS soon as Mrs Noah returned from the ark with Stumpy, she harnessed the elephant to the muddy tractor. Stumpy tossed his head, trumpeted loudly and heaved. He pulled and he pulled until the tractor shifted and rolled forward with a loud squelch. Water poured from every part of it. The tractor looked so miserable with pondweed stuck around its wheels and mud dripping from its lights, that Stumpy felt quite sorry for it. The elephant sucked up a trunkful of water and sprayed the tractor clean.

"Oh, thank you Stumpy!" cried Mrs Noah. "Now we just need Mr Sparks to come and check the engine."

Mr Sparks was soon on his way, carrying his bag of tools and a big can of oil. Noddy had found him at the garage, mending a little green pixie car. When Noddy told him about the tractor and the sheep the mechanic shook his head and frowned. Mr Sparks knew all about the shiny red tractor – he had sold it to Farmer Straw only a few weeks before!

NODDY FOUND MR SPARKS AT THE GARAGE, MENDING
A LITTLE GREEN PIXIE CAR

Now that Mr Sparks was ready to help, Noddy turned back to the farm. As he walked he wondered where all the missing animals could be. On the way back, Noddy crossed the village green. He hurried past some bushes, then stopped suddenly. Behind one of them, stood a funny, fluffy, white shape.

'Is that a little cloud?' wondered Noddy. 'No, clouds live up in the sky!'

Then he spied another woolly shape peeping out from behind a tree.

"It can't be the sheep again," he said out loud this time. "I put them all back in the field and shut the gate."

What could they be?

"Oink!" said one of the white woolly shapes.

"Who are you?" called Noddy. "You can't be a pig because they aren't woolly but I've never heard a sheep say 'oink'!"

Noddy was in a muddle.

Another woolly-pig trotted up to him, twirling its curly tail. "Oink!"

"How many of you are there?" asked Noddy.

A third woolly-pig appeared from behind a bush. Then another wandered out from under a holly tree. Its woolly coat was so tangled by the prickly leaves, it had nearly got stuck!

"Let me count you," said Noddy. "One, two, three. Oh, do keep still! I'll have to start all over again."

It took a full five minutes to round the animals up and count them properly! There were nine woolly-pigs in all.

"I don't know where you've come from, but Mrs Noah or Farmer Straw might," decided Noddy. "They know everything about animals."

Noddy started to walk on towards the farm, calling behind him.

"Follow me, woolly-pigs! Follow your new friend Noddy."

5

BEWARE OF THE GOBLINS

THE confused flock of woolly-pigs were happy to follow Noddy. They really wanted to go home to their muddy field and comfortable sties. They were hungry too and each one trotted behind, hoping that Noddy might have some food in his pocket. As they went along, Noddy started to sing.

> *"Oh, I found some sheep,*
> *And a tractor sunk deep,*
> *Now I've found woolly-pigs!*
> *Or are they oinky-sheep?"*

Noddy and the woolly-pigs had not gone far when they were startled by a loud squeak! Noddy reeled round in surprise.

"Squeak, squeak!" cried a little mouse, as he scampered past with his wife and children.

"Whatever is the matter?" asked Noddy.

The father mouse stopped to point a tiny paw.

"The goblins," he squeaked. "The goblins are going to do magic!"

Before the mouse family could scurry a step further, the sound of noisy laughter echoed around the trees.

"Ha ha, ha!" It rang. "Hee, hee, hee!"

Noddy already knew it had to be Sly and Gobbo.

A very cross beetle suddenly scuttled out from behind a tree stump. The goblins had turned her bright pink! She was looking for somewhere to hide in case a hungry bird saw her bright new colour and ate her.

Noddy's bell began to ring crossly.

'How dare those goblins do that to a beetle?' he thought. 'How dare they scare a family of mice away from their home?' Noddy stamped his foot. "Sly and Gobbo, come out at once!" he shouted.

Everything was quiet and still and then…

"…BOO!"

Noddy and the animals jumped with surprise as the two goblins popped out from behind the tree stump.

Noddy was rather afraid, but he tried not to show it.

"Sly and Gobbo," he frowned. "You have been very naughty – I am going to take you to Mr Plod the policeman!"

The goblins looked at Noddy and then at the woolly-pigs. Gobbo and Sly didn't look at all sorry.

Just as they started to laugh again, Farmer Straw's cockerel strutted up with Big-Ears at his side.

"Cock-a-doodle-do, what a to-do!" he crowed.

"Goblins!" roared Big-Ears. "What have you been up to?" Noddy's bell rang with relief. He knew his best friend would know exactly what to do with the naughty pair. In fact, Big-Ears was the only person in Toyland that Sly and Gobbo were scared of.

"Excuse me, sir," squeaked the mother mouse. "Noddy saved us and made the goblins come out of their hiding place."

Big-Ears beamed at Noddy. "Well done! That was very brave of you."

Noddy was so happy he gave Big-Ears a big hug.

NODDY AND THE ANIMALS JUMPED WITH SURPRISE

6

MR PLOD'S PROBLEM

SLY and Gobbo glared as Noddy told Big-Ears all about finding the sheep and the tractor. He also explained about the strange woolly-pigs.

"Well," said Big-Ears. "I think we should take these two back to the farm so that we can tell Farmer Straw what's been going on."

Big-Ears grasped Sly and Gobbo's hands firmly, then followed after Noddy and the woolly-pigs. With the cockerel strutting along at the back, they made a funny little procession!

Meanwhile, Mr Plod the policeman was cycling to the railway station as fast as he could. He could hear all kinds of mooing, laughter and barking coming from the platform. The puzzled policeman couldn't imagine what was going on.

'Stations are for trains and nothing else,' he thought sternly.

Mr Plod was very out of breath by the time he got to the ticket office.

"Now then," he roared. "What is going on here?"

The policeman gasped. The station was over-run by a mooing herd of cows! A crowd of dolls and toy soldiers had gathered round to point and stare. Not one of them had ever seen a blue cow before!

In amongst them, Farmer Straw's bull was snorting and Bumpy Dog was barking as loudly as he could.

Mr Plod took a deep breath and blew on his whistle. "Pheeeeeeeee!"

The whole platform went quiet, but before the policeman could say another word, he found himself pushed to the ground. He looked up to find Bumpy Dog licking him with a very wet tongue.

"Get off Bumpy Dog!" shouted Mr Plod.

A toy soldier stepped forward and helped him back to his feet. Bumpy Dog slipped away with his head down and his tail tucked between his legs.

Mr Plod took out his notebook and began to write. As he scribbled, Mr Wobbly-Man rolled forward.

"Have you seen what colour the cows are?" he asked.

Mr Plod did not look up. He was too busy writing to be interrupted.

"NOW THEN, WHAT IS GOING ON HERE?" ROARED MR PLOD

The bull snorted very loudly.

This time Mr Plod did look up. The poor man rubbed his eyes – suddenly noticing that every cow in front of him was really very blue!

"Who did this?" he demanded.

"Mr Plod sir," answered Mr Wobbly-Man. "I saw two goblins disappearing into some bushes as I passed the village green."

Mr Plod sucked his pencil.

"Yes," he agreed. "They are the only ones who can do magic. They must have turned the cows blue."

 The bull stamped his hooves and snorted again – he thought it was time someone helped the unhappy herd! He was also very cross that everyone had laughed at them.

Mr Plod looked at the cows and rubbed his chin. He knew that they ought to go back to the farm, but he wasn't sure that he could lead them all.

Suddenly, there was a loud whistle and the train puffed up to the platform.

Now Mr Plod knew just what to do. He would put the animals on the train and ask the driver to stop at the farm.

SUDDENLY THERE WAS A LOUD WHISTLE AND THE TRAIN
PUFFED UP TO THE PLATFORM

- 7 -

ALL ABOARD FOR THE FARM

MR Plod went up to the front of the train and spoke to the driver.

Next he turned to the bull and said, "How would you like a ride home?"

The bull snorted, but stepped forward and stomped onto the train. The blue cows looked at each other, then one bravely stepped into the first carriage. None of them had ever been on a train before and they weren't sure they wanted to now. But with the bull bellowing encouragement they each started to climb on. When the last blue cow had finally found a carriage to squeeze into, the engine heaved out of the station.

THE TRAIN WHISTLED MERRILY AS IT CHUFFED
THROUGH TOYLAND

The train whistled merrily as it chuffed through Toyland with its unusual load of passengers. The train had never carried farmyard animals before! The cows stared out of the carriages, mooing with surprise as the wind blew their ears around their heads. They could not believe how quickly the fields and meadows went past – if only they could run this fast, they would have such fun!

Before long the animals began to enjoy themselves. The bull tossed his head to wave at the rabbits who were watching the train puff by. He felt very grand standing in the front carriage next to Mr Plod and his bicycle.

The train rushed on, whistling at every corner. It chuffed through Bouncing Ball Town. The cows thought it would be great fun to live there if they could play with the balls all day. The bull looked out and saw Rocking Horse Town. He bellowed noisily – challenging the cantering horses to a race some time! The sun shone and a warm wind blew. The cows mooed with pleasure to think they would soon be home.

Back at the farm Mr Sparks, Mrs Noah and Stumpy the Elephant were busy fixing the tractor. They looked very startled when Noddy, Big-Ears, the goblins, the woolly-pigs and the cockerel walked through the farm gate.

"What are they?" asked Mrs Noah, pointing at the white, furry animals walking with Noddy. "I know every creature in Toyland, but I've never seen one of those."

"They are woolly-pigs," said Noddy. "They are fluffy like sheep but they have curly tails."

Big-Ears led the goblins up to Mrs Noah. She looked at the woolly-pigs and then shook her head.

"Sly and Gobbo," she said sternly. "You did this, didn't you?"

The goblins nodded their heads. Big-Ears made sure that he still had a firm hold of their hands.

Mr Sparks climbed onto the tractor seat. He turned the engine on, but it could only give a few half-hearted chugs.

"You need some more oil," said Mr Sparks.

Stumpy the Elephant used his trunk to pass up the can of oil.

When Mr Sparks tried the engine again, it started without coughing. The mechanic looked down at the naughty goblins.

"You're lucky that I could mend this," he scolded. "Farmer Straw would have been very angry to find his brand new tractor had been broken."

- 8 -

A SURPRISE FOR FARMER STRAW

"CHOO, choo!" Noddy, Big-Ears, Mrs Noah, Mr Sparks and Stumpy looked at each other in surprise.

"Why is the Toyland train stopping here?" asked Noddy. The friends peered down the hill to see a very strange crowd climbing off the train. There was Mr Plod and his bicycle, Farmer Straw's bull and what were they?

Noddy gasped when he realised that Mr Plod and the bull were leading a herd of blue cows up the field! Mr Plod was very out of breath by the time they all made it into the farmyard.

"What?" he panted. "Are you all doing here?"

The farm was very crowded and everyone started talking, mooing, baaing and oinking at once. No one heard Farmer Straw's horse and cart rattling up to the gate. He was most surprised to come home to such an unruly gathering.

"What's going on here?" he roared over the din. Everyone jumped to see the farmer back from the market.

Noddy, Mr Plod and Mr Sparks rushed forward and began to explain.

THE FRIENDS PEERED DOWN THE HILL TO SEE A VERY
STRANGE CROWD CLIMBING OFF THE TRAIN

Noddy told Farmer Straw about the sheep, the goblins and the woolly-pigs. Mr Plod explained how the blue cows were found and brought back to the farm and then Mr Sparks showed him the tractor.

"Well, well," said Farmer Straw, looking at Sly and Gobbo. "You have been up to mischief."

The goblins looked at each other and blushed.

"We are sorry…" they both said quietly.

"Woof, woof, woof!"

It was Bumpy Dog. He scampered through the gate with a flock of hens and a line of ducks waddling behind him. Everyone cheered to see all the animals safely back where they belonged. Nobody even minded when Bumpy Dog launched himself at Noddy and Big-Ears, licking them until they were wet all over.

No one ever did find out where the hens and ducks had been all day. Their little adventure stayed a secret, even to the farm cockerel.

- 9 -

HOORAY FOR NODDY!

ONCE he was sure that all the animals were safe, Farmer Straw turned his attention back to Sly and Gobbo.

The goblins gulped nervously. What was he going to say?

"You two have done some bad things today," frowned the farmer. "I could have lost all my animals and you might have ruined my tractor. Thank goodness Noddy and his friends were here to put everything right! I am going to give a party to thank everyone for their help. We'll have it in the field tonight!"

The farmyard echoed with cheers. Everyone rushed away to tell their friends about the party. As soon as he got home, Noddy told Tessie Bear all about his adventures. She thought Noddy had been so brave she decided to make a cake for the occasion.

Gobbo and Sly tried to slink away too, but Stumpy caught them in his trunk.

"You two," said Farmer Straw, "can sweep the farmyard, clean the pig sties, muck out Stamper's stable and tidy the barn. No magic!"

Suddenly the bull bellowed, the blue cows mooed and the woolly-pigs oinked angrily.

"And Goblins!" added Farmer Straw. "You will turn the cows brown again and give the pigs their pink, bristly coats back."

"Oh alright," groaned Gobbo.

There was a small crack and a puff of green smoke. In an instant the cows became brown again and the pigs lost their woolly coats.

Before they could make any excuses, brushes were thrust into the goblins' hands. The sorry pair scrubbed, swept and cleaned for a long time. They were so tired when they finished, they could hardly stand up!

Farmer Straw checked all over the farm and then smiled.

"You did make a mess today, but now you've made the farm sparkle!" he began. "If you promise to behave, you can come to the party."

The goblins clapped their hands with delight and nodded as hard as they could. Of course they would behave!

By tea-time everything was set for the party. The animals from the ark filed first through the gate, proudly led by Stumpy. Noddy, Tessie Bear and Big-Ears came next, followed by all their friends.

The guests played blind man's buff and musical chairs. Stumpy won the musical chairs because everyone was scared the elephant might sit on them by mistake. Next they played pass the parcel and everybody got a present.

A long table was piled high with buns, jam tarts, sausage rolls and all kinds of treats. There were trifles, jellies and large jugs of lemonade. Right in the middle was Tessie Bear's cake, covered in pink icing. It was enormous – she had even decorated it with sugar sheep, pigs and cows! Everyone thought she had been ever so clever.

When it started to grow dark, bright lanterns were hung around the field. At the end of the feast, Farmer Straw and Noddy cut the cake as everybody clapped and cheered.

As the slices were passed round to the happy guests, a flurry of red, green, gold and blue fireworks lit the sky. Big-Ears nudged his friend and beamed. The colourful sparkles high up in the sky spelled out the words

'THANK YOU!'

'David Bellamy's

Winter

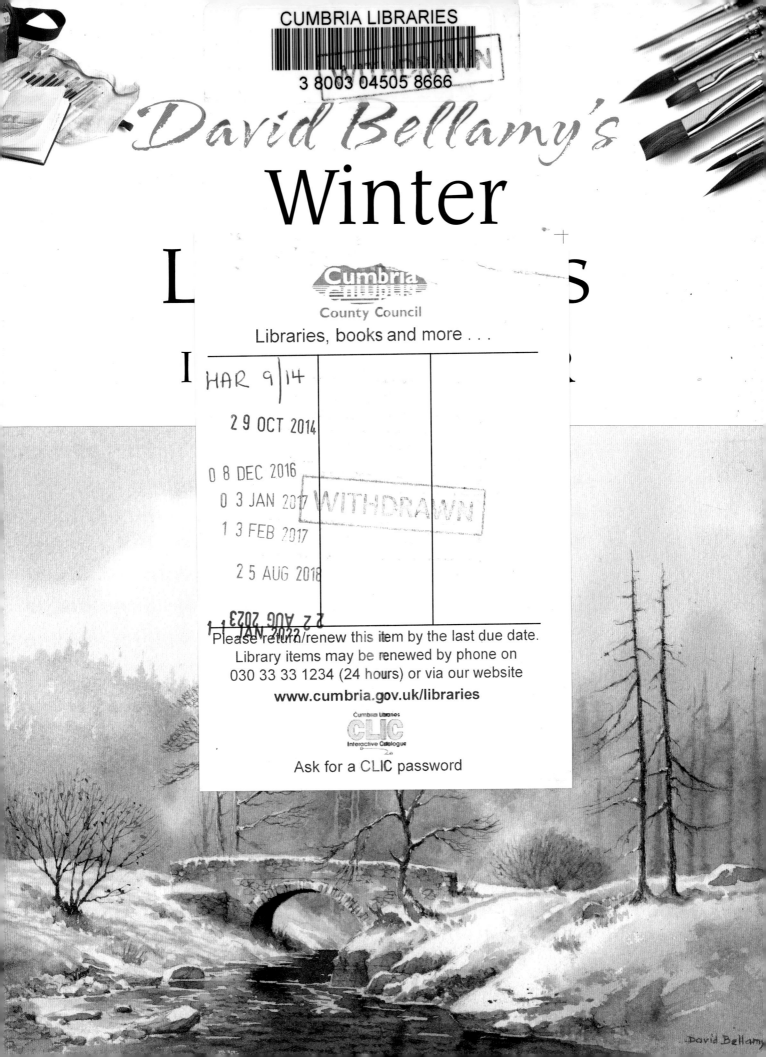

David Bellamy

Dedication
To those hardy companions who, over the years, have endured appalling winter conditions, uncomplaining, while I complete an equally appalling sketch.